Book 3

All-Star Cheerleaders

Just So, Brianna

All-Star Cheerleaders

Book #1 Tick Tock, Taylor!

Book #2 Save the Best for Last, Abby

Book #3 Just So, Brianna

Do your best and forget the rest!

For Jill

Kane Miller, A Division of EDC Publishing

Text copyright © Anastasia Suen 2011
Illustrations copyright © Kane Miller 2011

For information contact:
Kane Miller, A Division of EDC Publishing
PO Box 470663
Tulsa, OK 74147-0663
www.kanemiller.com
www.edcpub.com
www.usbornebooksandmore.com

Library of Congress Control Number: 2011933992

Printed in the United States of America

1 2 3 4 5 6 7 8 9 10

ISBN: 978-1-61067-002-9

Book 3

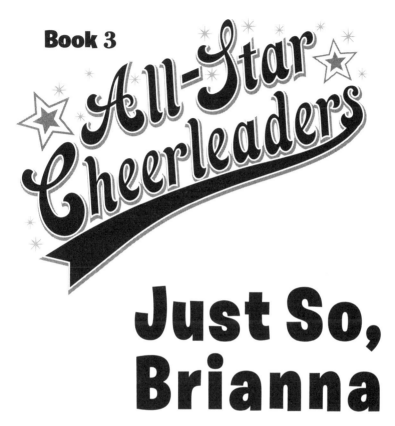

All-Star Cheerleaders

Just So, Brianna

Written by Anastasia Suen
Illustrated by Hazel Mitchell

Kane Miller
A DIVISION OF EDC PUBLISHING

Saturday

Six-year-old Brianna heard laughing. *What are they doing now?* She ran to the bedroom window and looked out. Her big sister Hannah was having a party in the backyard with her friends. They were all on the same All-Star cheerleading squad, the Stars, at the Big D Elite Gym.

Brianna was an All-Star cheerleader too. But her squad was much smaller. They only had eight girls. The mini squad was named

Glitter. Coach Tammy called them her Glitter girls.

Hannah's youth squad had twenty girls. Not all of them were in the backyard, but almost. At the gym, the Stars filled the entire room when they performed. They could do lots of fancy moves.

Brianna loved to watch the stunts they did. You needed bases and flyers to do stunts. A base was a girl who held up a flyer. The flyer did a pose in the air. It looked so nice when they all did it together.

Brianna watched from the upstairs window as the girls lifted her sister Hannah.

Hannah is a flyer just like me. Brianna smiled. *I love to fly. It's so pretty.*

Hannah lifted one leg into the air. The bases held on to her other leg so she wouldn't fall. Hannah held her foot above her head. She pointed her toe at the sky. Then she lifted her other arm into the air for a high V.

Nice heel stretch, thought Brianna.

Then Hannah let go of her foot. She put her leg back into her bases' hands. The other girls brought Hannah back down to the grass.

I want to watch this up close. Brianna ran down the stairs. She opened the door and went out into the backyard. The big girls all turned and looked at her.

"There's our Baby Star," said Samantha.

"I was wondering where you were," said Jada.

"Come over here, Bebe," said Hannah.

When Brianna was a baby she couldn't say her name. She called herself Bebe. Everyone in the family still called her that. Brianna walked over and stood next to Hannah.

"Hailey isn't here yet," said Hannah. "And we want to keep practicing. You can take her place until she comes."

"OK, Hannah," said Brianna. She acted

calm on the outside. Inside she did a little cheer. *Yay! I can fly with the big girls!*

"Really?" said Victoria. "The baby can fly?" She looked down at Brianna as if she didn't believe it.

Brianna looked over at Victoria. *I'll show you what I can do.*

Victoria didn't know Brianna well. She didn't know that Brianna practiced every move until it was perfect. Brianna did everything just so.

"Claire, Padma, Lauren and Samantha will be your bases," said Hannah.

"Over here," said Samantha. She waved her hand.

Brianna walked over to where her bases were standing. There were five groups of bases lined up in a row. They reached from one side of the lawn to the other.

"Stand here," said Samantha. "We'll count to eight and then lift you up."

"I know," said Brianna. "That's how we do it too. What moves are the flyers doing?"

"Liberty prep and then scale," said Samantha. "Can you do those?"

"Sure," said Brianna.

"OK," said Samantha. "Here we go. Five, six, seven, eight."

The girls lifted Brianna. She went up faster and higher than she usually did. The girls on Hannah's squad were taller than the girls on her squad. The Stars were nine, ten and eleven years old. The girls on Brianna's Glitter squad were only six, seven and eight years old.

"Now do a liberty prep," said Samantha. But she was too late. Brianna already had her left knee out in front of her. And her arms were already lifted up into a high V. Brianna always did everything just so. Everything always had to be perfect.

"Now do a scale," said Samantha, and she started counting again. "Five, six, seven, eight."

Brianna moved her left knee out to her side. Then she reached down and grabbed her leg. She pulled her leg up and over and held on.

Her right arm was still up in the air. But now her left leg made the other side of the V. *That was easy.*

Brianna glanced over at her sister. *We're flying together! It's so pretty, all of us in a row. I'm one of the big girls!*

Then she looked under Hannah. There was Victoria, holding Hannah up. *Miss Bossy is only a base. Humph! What does she know about flying?*

"And down," said Samantha. Brianna put her legs and arms together. The bases brought her back down. Then the girls ran across the grass. Brianna followed them. *What are they going to do now?*

Brianna watched as Hannah did three back handsprings across the grass.

I wish I could do that, thought Brianna. *Maybe when I'm a Star...*

Then Padma, Claire and Samantha started their cartwheels.

I can do cartwheels, thought Brianna. Then she looked again. They were doing them with one hand!

Down, up and over. They did three cartwheels in a row. But only one hand touched the ground.

That looks so pretty, thought Brianna. *I want to do that too.*

Me Too!

"You can do cartwheels, can't you?" said Jada.

"Of course," said Brianna.

"OK," said Jada. "Follow me. Start yours when I'm halfway across the grass."

Brianna nodded her head. "I can do that."

Jada started counting. "Five, six, seven, eight."

Jada did her cartwheel.

Whoa! Another one-handed cartwheel. I want to try that.

Brianna watched as Jada moved across the yard. *She's halfway there. It's my turn.*

Brianna put her hand on the grass and started her cartwheel. *One.*

Then she put her other hand down. *Two. No, wait, I'm not supposed to use that hand! It's too late. I'd better keep going.*

Brianna lifted her legs into the air. *Three, four.*

Now over and down. Five, six, seven.

Brianna put her arms up. *Eight.*

Now for the next one, but with one *hand this time!*

Brianna started her next cartwheel.

First hand down. One.

Hold the other hand out. Two.

Big kick, legs up. Three, four.

And over. Five, six, seven.

Eight. Brianna lifted both hands into the

air. *Now one more. Can I do it again?*

Brianna started her third cartwheel.

First hand down. One.

Hold the other hand out. Two.

Big kick and ... whoa!

Brianna flipped forward and landed on her knees.

"Ha, ha, ha!"

Is someone laughing? Who is laughing?

Brianna stood up and looked at the girls standing by the fence.

"Ha, ha, ha!"

It's Victoria.

"It wasn't that bad," said Jada.

"She fell over doing a cartwheel! That's *so* easy," said Victoria. She started laughing again.

"All right, all right, that's enough," said Hannah.

Victoria snickered, so Hannah glared at her. "Just stop."

"Fine," said Victoria. She crossed her arms and looked away.

"It was pretty good for a tiny," said Samantha.

"I'm not a tiny," said Brianna.

Hannah came over and stood next to Brianna. "She's a mini, now."

"Our Baby Star is a mini Star," said Claire.

"She's just a tiny, uh, mini version of you, Hannah," said Padma. "So cute."

Brianna smiled. She loved it when people said she was like Hannah.

"It's not cute," said Victoria, "that she can't even do the moves."

Victoria pointed her finger at Brianna. "Falling down isn't cute. It's stupid. That's not how you win."

"Victoria!" said Hannah.

"What?" said Victoria. "You know I'm right."

Brianna frowned. *You're mean.*

"Enough of this," said Victoria. She waved her hand in the air. "Let's go practice the next stunt."

"That's why we're here," said Hannah. "It's a cheer party! Food, friends and cheer. What else could a girl want?"

"Boys!" said Jada.

The big girls laughed as they walked across the grass. Brianna watched the big girls follow her sister ... and Victoria. They all walked back to the middle of the yard. Victoria's ponytail almost reached her waist.

You're pretty on the outside, thought Brianna, *but not on the inside. Mommy says that pretty girls are pretty inside and out. And you're not.*

Brianna crossed her arms. *I'll show you I can do it. I'll show you how to be pretty.*

Hannah turned around and waved at Brianna. "Come on, Bebe. We need you to fly."

"Coming," said Brianna, and she ran across the grass.

Tuesday Practice

There she is. Emma's finally here. Brianna ran across the mat at the Big D Elite Gym. "Emma, Emma, guess what I did," said Brianna.

"What?" said Emma. She was six and a flyer just like Brianna.

"Oh, we just have to try it," said Brianna.

Emma walked over to the edge of the mat and put her backpack down. "Try what?"

"A one-handed cartwheel," said Brianna.

"What!" said Emma. She stared at Brianna.

"I can't do that. I always fall over."

"I know," said Brianna. She shook her head. "That's what I did at Hannah's party. Well, I didn't fall over *every* time, but almost."

"At Hannah's party!" said Emma. "They let you cheer with them?"

"They did," said Brianna. She jumped up and down and clapped her hands. "Hailey was late, so they let me fly."

Emma grabbed Brianna's arm. "You got to fly with the Stars squad?"

"I did," said Brianna. "And they lifted me so high."

Emma lifted her hand toward the ceiling. "Of course! They're so much taller."

"I know," said Brianna.

"What else did they let you do?" asked Emma. "Tell me, tell me!"

"First I did a liberty prep," said Brianna. "Then I did a scale."

"A scale! Up so high?" said Emma.

"Well, I can do it down low," said Brianna. "So I had to try it."

"Did you wobble?" asked Emma. "I always feel like I'm going to fall over when I get up that high."

Brianna shook her head. "No, I didn't wobble there …" And then she looked down at the mat.

"Uh-oh," said Emma. She put her hand on Brianna's arm. "Tell me what happened."

"She laughed at me!" said Brianna.

"Who?" asked Emma.

"Victoria," said Brianna.

"Who is Victoria?" said Emma.

"The one with hair down to her waist," said Brianna. She touched her back to show how long it was.

"Wow," said Emma. "That's long! It must be pretty."

"Oh, it is," said Brianna. "She's pretty

on the outside. But not on the inside. She's mean." Brianna closed her eyes.

"What did she do?" asked Emma.

"She laughed at me," said Brianna. "Hannah had to make her stop."

"Why?" said Emma.

"I fell when I was doing the one-handed cartwheel," said Brianna.

"But that's a hard move," said Emma. "I can't do it yet."

"I did it once," said Brianna. "And then I fell down." She made a fist and raised it in the air. "I'm going to practice it until it's perfect! I'll show her!"

So Perfect

Brianna looked around the gym. Not everyone was there yet. Coach Tammy was talking to some of the mothers. They were standing by the door.

"Let's do it now," said Brianna, "before Coach Tammy starts practice."

"OK," said Emma.

The two flyers walked over to the edge of the big blue mat. It covered almost all of the floor in the gym.

"Here I go," said Brianna.

She pulled her left arm in. Then she raised her right arm.

Right hand down on the mat. One.

Keep your left hand off *the mat. Two.*

Kick hard, legs up. Three, four.

And over.

Whomp! Brianna fell forward on the mat.

Not again!

"What are you doing on the floor?" asked Sophia.

Not Sophia! Brianna turned around. *Sophia never has anything nice to say. She is just like Victoria.*

"What does it look like?" said Emma.

"Like she fell over," said Sophia. "Your timing is way off."

"And you're so perfect," said Brianna. "You never fall."

"No, I don't," said Sophia. She looked down at Brianna. "You need to practice

more. You'll never get better if you don't practice."

Brianna looked at Emma. Emma shrugged.

"That's what happens when you practice," said Brianna. "You fall down. Duh!"

"Well, I don't," said Sophia. "I never fall."

Never fall? Yeah, right. Brianna shook her head. Girls fell at practice all the time. No one was that perfect.

Coach Tammy walked across the mat. "What's going on over here?"

"Cartwheels," said Emma.

"I tried to do a one-handed cartwheel," said Brianna.

"And she made a mess of it," said Sophia.

"Now, Sophia," said Coach Tammy. "You know it takes time to learn something new."

Coach Tammy turned to face the other girls on the mat. Then she clapped her hands three times. **Clap, clap, clap!**

"Let's warm up, Glitter girls. Then we can practice one-handed cartwheels."

Yes, thought Brianna. *Yes!*

CHAPTER 5
At Last

On Thursday afternoon, Brianna opened the door to the gym. *I hope I can do the one-handed cartwheel right today. I really want to do it like Hannah's squad does.*

Brianna walked inside and put down her backpack. She looked around, but Emma wasn't there yet. *Uh-oh, there's Sophia.*

"You were terrible last time," said Sophia. "Why don't you do your cartwheels with two hands? It looks bad when you fall."

Brianna looked up at Sophia. *Why is she so mean?*

Sophia was eight, so she had been on the Glitter squad for almost three years. But she never seemed to have anything nice to say.

"I didn't fall on purpose," said Brianna.

"But you did," said Sophia. "Over and over again."

"I'm practicing," said Brianna. "Just like you said."

"Well, stop," said Sophia. "It looks ugly." Then she walked away.

No, you stop! Stop being so ugly. Why don't you leave me alone? Brianna sat down and opened her backpack. She took out her water bottle and took a sip. *I'm not ugly, I'm pretty. The one-handed cartwheel is pretty too. I can do it.*

Brianna looked up. *Emma! At last!*

Emma came over and put down her backpack. She gave Brianna a hug. "I saw

Sophia talking to you."

They both looked over at the other side of the mat. Sophia was wagging her finger at Kayla, now.

"She's so bossy," said Emma.

"I know," replied Brianna. She shook her head. "But we can do the one-handed cartwheel. Can't we?"

"Well, not every time yet," said Emma. "But we'll keep practicing it. We'll show her."

"Yes, we will," said Brianna. "We'll show Sophia." Brianna put her water bottle in her backpack.

Clap, clap, clap!

Coach Tammy clapped her hands. It was time to start.

Everyone warmed up, and then the girls practiced their routine. After the second time, Coach Tammy looked over at Brianna. "Let's try that one-handed cartwheel again. It's a Level 1 skill everyone needs to know."

"Yay!" Brianna jumped up and grabbed Emma's hand.

"But they can't do it," said Sophia.

"Sophia," said Coach Tammy, "let me do the coaching." Then she turned to face Brianna and Emma.

"When you do a one-handed cartwheel, you need to give it a little extra kick. Let me show you." Coach Tammy walked to the far side of the mat. Then she started her one-handed cartwheel.

"One hand down." Coach Tammy put her hand down. "Let the lines on the mat help you."

She put her hand on the white line, thought Brianna. *I can do that.*

"Keep your other arm out to the side," said Coach Tammy.

That's the tricky part, thought Brianna. *I'm used to putting both hands down.*

"Then a strong kick," said Coach Tammy.

Brianna watched as Coach Tammy's legs

went up and over.

Maybe that's what's wrong, thought Brianna. *Maybe I'm not kicking hard enough.*

"And come up." Coach Tammy lifted her arms into the air.

It's not that different, thought Brianna. *Hands down. No, one hand down. The other hand out. Then up and over.*

"Now you try it," said Coach Tammy. "Line up over there." She pointed to the far side of the mat.

Brianna went over and stood at the back of the line. *I want to see how everyone else does it.*

One by one, the Glitter girls gave it a try. Abby, Taylor and Kayla all did it quite easily.

Then it was Sophia's turn. *It looks so easy when Sophia does it,* thought Brianna. *It looks perfect.* She sighed.

Then Sophia turned around and looked at Brianna.

I see you, thought Brianna. *Show off.*

Maddie and Liv also did it without any problem. Now only the two flyers were left.

Then Emma did her cartwheel. She fell down halfway.

Oh, Emma!

"Try it again," said Coach Tammy. "Kick a little harder."

"OK," said Emma. She went back and did it again.

Brianna watched as Emma went down, up and over.

She didn't fall! If she can do it, I can do it too. We're best friends.

Emma turned around and gave Brianna a thumbs up.

Here I go! I have to remember that big kick.

Brianna started her cartwheel.

One hand down,

the other hand out,

big kick,

up and over.

Both hands in the air.

Coach Tammy started clapping.

What?

"Congratulations," said Coach Tammy. "I knew you two could do it."

Brianna turned around and looked at Emma. *Perfect! We did it!* The two friends grinned and hugged each other.

CHAPTER 6

In the Car

On Saturday morning, Brianna's mom drove them to the competition. Brianna sat in the back seat between Padma and Claire. Hannah sat in the front seat like she always did. The youth squad didn't cheer until after lunch. The mothers took turns driving them to practice. The other mothers would come later to see them cheer.

The younger girls always competed first. The littlest ones were called tinies. They were only three, four and five years old. When Brianna was a tiny, she had to be there very early. Sometimes they did their warm-up at 7:30 in the morning. That was early!

Now that she was a mini, Brianna usually warmed up at 8:00 or 8:30. That was still pretty early in the morning. She had to get dressed, eat breakfast and get in the car for the long drive before that. No time for cartoons on a Saturday. It was like a school morning. Hurry, hurry, hurry.

Brianna recited the one-handed cartwheel steps to herself as they rode in the car. She wanted everything to be perfect. "Right hand down. One. Left hand out. Two."

"What are you saying?" asked Claire.

"My moves," said Brianna.

"Oh, Hannah, your little sister is just so cute," said Padma.

"She takes after me," said Hannah.

The big girls laughed. Padma reached over and hugged Brianna.

I want to be on Hannah's squad, thought Brianna. *The big girls are so nice. They get to do all of the pretty moves. Everything is just so. It all looks so perfect.*

I want to be perfect like that too. Brianna sighed. She always worried on competition days. *Everyone will be looking at me. What if I make a mistake? What will people say?*

"Have you been practicing your one-handed cartwheels?" asked Claire.

Brianna nodded.

"It's a little slow," said Hannah. "But minis aren't that fast."

"I was fast when I was a mini," said Padma.

"So was I," said Claire.

Brianna looked at Hannah. *But I'm not fast …*

"Well," said Hannah, "sometimes you have to slow down to get it right." She reached over and patted Brianna's knee. "I'm sure she'll be just fine."

"We'll be right next to you, cheering you on," said Claire.

"You will?" asked Brianna.

"Of course," said Padma. "They put the performance mat up on a stage at this convention center. It's not like the other ones where the mat is on the floor. There we have to stand by the wall so everyone else can see you."

"When they let you cheer up on a stage," said Claire, "we can come right up to the edge of the mat and cheer you on."

"We'll all be there," said Hannah.

You will! Brianna grinned from ear to ear. *It's going to be a great day!*

And Now It Begins

Brianna's mom drove the car up the driveway in front of the convention center. She parked the car by one of the doors. "I'll drop you girls off here and go find a parking space. Make sure you bring in your backpacks. I can't carry them all in by myself."

Hannah laughed. "That would be funny!"

"Oh, you!" said her mom.

"Just kidding!" said Hannah. She leaned

over and gave her mom a kiss. "Thanks, Mom."

"Thanks, Mrs. G.," said Padma, from the back seat.

"Thank you," said Claire.

"You're very welcome, girls. Hannah, please take Bebe to Coach Tammy."

"I will," said Hannah. "Come on, Bebe."

"We'll take good care of her, Mrs. G.," said Padma.

Brianna leaned into the front seat and gave her mom a kiss. Then she put on her backpack and got out of the car. Brianna stood on the sidewalk and looked up at the big building. Then she looked back down the street. The convention center was two blocks long! *I hope I don't get lost in there.*

Hannah reached out and took Brianna's hand. "Let's go find Coach Tammy," said Hannah.

Brianna walked into the building with Hannah and the big girls. Hannah walked up to the desk and asked, "Where is Big D Elite?"

The lady at the desk looked down at her notebook. Then she pointed at a long hallway. It was filled with people. "Down that hall," said the lady. "You can't miss it."

Are you sure? thought Brianna. *That's a lot of people.*

"Thanks," said Hannah. "Let's go, Bebe." Hannah held on to Brianna's hand.

The girls walked down the crowded hallway. There were moms and dads, grandmothers and grandfathers. There were lots of cheerleaders everywhere.

"All these squads think they're the best," said Claire.

"But they're not," said Padma.

"Big D Elite ..." said Hannah.

Brianna and the other girls joined in. "...

can't be beat. We're the ones you want to meet!"

As they finished their cheer, the girls reached the end of the long hallway. Brianna saw a sign on the second door. It said *Big D Elite.*

"Look, there's our name on the door," said Brianna.

"Under a star," said Claire.

"But of course," said Padma.

"They know we're the Stars," said Hannah. The big girls laughed as they walked in the door. Girls of all ages from the Big D Elite Gym were getting ready.

"I see Coach Tammy," said Brianna.

"I'll take you over," said Hannah. "I promised Mom."

A promise is a promise. Brianna and the girls walked across the room to where the minis were getting ready.

Hannah knelt down and hugged Brianna. "You can do it, Bebe."

"OK," said Brianna. She nodded her head. *If Hannah said it, then it must be true. She's been cheering for a long time. Ever since I was a baby!*

"We'll be rooting for you," said Padma.

"Go get 'em!" said Claire.

Brianna watched as the big girls joined the rest of the youth squad. The girls on the Stars squad were putting makeup on each other. *Someday I'll be a Star too. I'll be perfect just like they are. See how pretty they are … and they aren't even worried about the competition. They're just having fun!*

Sophia came up behind Brianna. "You think you're so good just because your sister's a Star."

What? Brianna turned around and looked up at Sophia. *I didn't say anything to her. Why is she so mean to me?*

CHAPTER 8
Getting Ready

"Brianna," said Coach Tammy, "come and get your makeup on."

"Coming," said Brianna. She ran over and sat down in front of Coach Tammy. Brianna breathed a sigh of relief. *Sophia won't bother me now.*

"Close your eyes," said Coach Tammy.

Brianna closed her eyes. *I love this part. Now I'll be pretty just like the big girls. I'll be perfect ...*

Coach Tammy put silver-and-gold eye shadow on Brianna.

"Now pucker up," said Coach Tammy.

Brianna opened her eyes and puckered her lips. Coach Tammy put on the bright-red lipstick.

"Now everyone can see your beautiful smile," said Coach Tammy.

Brianna smiled. *Coach Tammy is so nice.*

"And here's your star," said Coach Tammy. She put a glittery star on Brianna's cheek.

"Now you're ready," said Coach Tammy. She hugged Brianna. "You look gorgeous."

Brianna hugged Coach Tammy tightly. *Now I feel better.*

Brianna looked over Coach Tammy's shoulder. There was Sophia, wagging her finger at Liv. *Why does Sophia have to be so mean?*

"Take off your warm-ups so we can go and practice," said Coach Tammy.

"OK," said Brianna. She unzipped her Big D Elite jacket. Then she took off her warm-up pants. She put them both in her backpack. Then she noticed her shoes.

My shoelaces are crooked! Brianna bent

down and retied her laces. *I don't want to look crooked. Everything has to be just right. It just has to be ...*

Coach Tammy clapped her hands three times. **Clap, clap, clap!**

"Glitter," said Coach Tammy. "Let's line up so we can go to the practice room."

Brianna looked around the room. *There's Emma!*

Brianna ran over and grabbed Emma's hand. The two flyers walked over to the Glitter girls' line.

The Glitter girls followed Coach Tammy out into the crowded hallway. Brianna looked at all the people in the hallway. Crowds made her nervous.

"There are so many people here," said Brianna.

"They all came to see us," said Emma.

"Oh," said Brianna. *That's right. They came to see us cheer. They're just here to watch us cheer.*

Brianna squeezed Emma's hand. "That's because we're so pretty when we cheer."

"Yes, we are," said Emma. She squeezed back.

Now the Glitter girls were on the other side of the convention center. They followed Coach Tammy down another long hallway. At the last door was a lady with a clipboard.

Coach Tammy led the Glitter girls up to the door. She took a sheet of paper out of her pocket and unfolded it. She showed it to the lady holding the clipboard. "This is Big D Elite Glitter. We have an 8:30 warm-up time."

The lady looked down at her clipboard. She wrote an X beside their squad name. "Come right in," she said. She pointed at the back wall. "The line starts over there."

Coach Tammy led the girls over to the far side of the room. They stood at the back of the line.

Brianna looked around the room. It was filled with cheerleaders. There were squads everywhere.

"Look at all the minis," said Brianna.

"They're our competition," said Emma.

"But they're not as pretty as we are," said Brianna.

Emma shook her head. "No, they're not."

Finally, it was Glitter's turn to practice. Brianna and Emma led the squad onto the mat. Coach Tammy turned on the music. After a few notes a deep voice said, "Presenting … Big D Elite Glitter." That was their cue! The Glitter girls began to move.

Brianna and Emma did the back limber together. Then they did their stunts. The other girls lifted them up into the air. They came down and did their jumps. Then it was time for the one-handed cartwheel.

Brianna and Emma walked to the edge of the mat. They waited for the other girls to go. Then it was Emma's turn. Brianna watched Emma do her cartwheel. One hand down and ...

Yes! She did it! Now it's my turn.

Brianna lifted her hands into the air. Then she put one hand down on the mat. A big kick and ... whomp!

Brianna fell.

Oh, no! Now what?

She looked up and saw Coach Tammy waving. "Keep going!"

Everyone is looking at me. Brianna stood up and did another cartwheel, with two hands this time. *No more falling over.*

Brianna did another cartwheel with two hands. Her last. She came up right next to Sophia.

Sophia leaned over and said, "I knew you couldn't do it."

Pep Talk

Brianna and Emma stood in line behind the curtain. The Glitter girls were going on the stage next. Music played on the other side as another squad did their routine.

"I can't believe I fell," said Brianna.

"It's OK," said Emma.

"No, it's not," said Brianna. "It was terrible."

"Coach Tammy wasn't upset," said Emma.

Brianna turned and looked back at the

line behind them. "But Sophia …"

Brianna turned back to face the curtain. *My cheering wasn't pretty. It was ugly!* Brianna began to cry.

Emma put her arm around Brianna. "Don't cry! You did your best."

No, I didn't, thought Brianna, and she cried even harder.

Emma looked around for Coach Tammy. But she was already on the other side of the curtain. She had gone out to give the crew their music.

We'll lose, thought Brianna, *all because of me.*

The Glitter girls came out of their line and stood around Brianna. "What's the matter?" asked Emma's big sister, Abby.

Everyone stop looking at me! Brianna cried even harder.

"Emma," said Abby. "What's going on?"

"Sophia," whispered Emma.

Abby shook her head. Then a large group of girls came up behind her. They were also wearing Big D Elite uniforms. It was the Stars!

"What's the matter, Bebe?" said Hannah. She put her arm around Brianna.

Hannah? Hannah is here? Brianna uncovered her face and looked up at her big sister. "I can't …" Brianna wailed.

"Can't what?" asked Hannah. But Brianna just kept crying.

"It's the one-handed cartwheel," said Emma. "She fell over."

"I can't do it!" wailed Brianna. "I just can't …" She looked over at Sophia. Then she started crying again.

"But that was just the warm-up," said Hannah. "It doesn't count, remember?"

Brianna stopped crying. She opened her eyes and looked up at her sister. "But I wanted it to be just so."

Hannah shook her head. "Practice doesn't have to be perfect." She pointed at the curtain. "The judges aren't back here. They can't see in the practice room, either. The judges didn't see anything."

Brianna looked at the curtain. *That's right. The judges are on the* other *side.*

Brianna listened to the music playing on the other side of the curtain. *The judges are watching the other girls. They didn't see my mistakes. They don't know I wasn't perfect.*

"You can do it," said Hannah. "I know you can. I saw it with my own two eyes."

"So did I," said Claire.

"Me too," said Padma.

"We all saw it at the party," said Samantha.

"Now dry your tears, Bebe," said Hannah. "We want you to be pretty for the judges."

I want to be pretty for the judges too, thought Brianna. *I want to be perfect.*

Hannah wiped away Brianna's tears. "You're our beautiful Bebe. You can do it."

Yes, thought Brianna. *Yes, I can.*

On Stage

The man standing next to the curtain looked at his watch. Then he looked at his clipboard. "Big D Elite," he said. "You're on!"

It's time to go on stage! Brianna took Emma's hand and led the Glitter girls. They went to the edge of the curtain. Then they walked up the steps and onto the stage.

Brianna looked into the stands and saw her mom. *She's waving!* Brianna smiled. *She knows I can do it!*

Brianna walked to her place on the mat and put her head down. The music started.

"Presenting … Big D Elite Glitter," said the deep voice.

Brianna lifted her head and looked over at Emma. They did the back limber together. They moved at the same time. It was perfect. *I can do it.*

After the other girls did their back limbers, it was time for stunts.

Taylor, Maddie and Liv lifted Brianna high in the air.

Brianna lifted her arms above her head. *Look how pretty I am.* Brianna smiled a very big smile.

Then the girls carried her over to the middle of the mat. Brianna reached out and touched Emma's hand. *We're both pretty.*

The Glitter girls brought both flyers down to the mat.

Here is our first cartwheel. Down and over I go!

One, two, three. Brianna did three cartwheels with the Glitter girls. *I did it. I can do it!*

Brianna ran to the front of the mat for the four jumps. *Five, six, seven, eight.* She jumped in the air and touched her toes. The entire squad turned and did it again and again and again.

Now we do the cartwheel circle. Brianna ran to her place. The Glitter girls made a circle in the middle of the mat. Then they did cartwheels out to the edge. *See, I can do cartwheels.*

Brianna ran over and stood next to Emma. The two flyers waited while the older girls did their running and tumbling. After Emma went, it was Brianna's turn.

I can do this, thought Brianna. *I can!* She started the first one-handed cartwheel.

One hand down,

the other hand out,

big kick,

up and over.

I did it!

Now two more.

One hand down,

the other hand out,

big kick,

up and over.

Two done!

Just one more …

One hand down,

the other hand out,

big kick,

up and over.

I did it! It was perfect!

Brianna heard clapping. She looked up. Hannah's squad was standing next to the stage. *They're clapping for me!*

Brianna smiled. Then she ran over to do

a thigh stand with Maddie. Maddie lifted Brianna in the air.

Brianna came back down. Taylor and Liv came over and lifted Brianna even higher. She did one more flyer move. Then the girls carried her across the mat again.

Brianna smiled even wider as she reached out and touched Emma's hand. *We are so pretty!*

Both flyers came down to the mat for the cheer.

As the Glitter girls started the chant, the other girls from Big D Elite joined in. Their voices filled the room.

"Big D Elite, can't be beat.

We're the ones you want to meet!"

The Glitter girls made another circle.

One, two, three, four and turn and step. Arms out.

Five, six, seven, eight, arms up.

And then it was time for the final stunt.

Brianna ran over to meet her bases. Taylor, Maddie and Liv lifted her into the air.

Brianna smiled as she held her hands high. She could see Hannah's squad standing next to the stage, cheering.

Yes! I did it.

"That's my beautiful Bebe," said Hannah.

Yes, I am.

About the Author

Books have always been part of Anastasia Suen's life. Her mother started reading to her when she was a baby and took her to the library every week. She wrote her first picture book when she was eleven and has been writing ever since. She used to be an elementary school teacher, and now she visits classrooms to talk about being an author. She has published over 130 books, writes an Internet blog about children's books and teaches writing to college students. She's never been a cheerleader, but she can yell really loud!